Why I Built the Boogle House

by

Helen Palmer

with photographs by

Lynn Fayman

BEGINNER BOOKS   A Division of Random House, Inc.

3 466

Why I Built the

Boogle House

Barry Barry

Carolyn Taylor

238 Elizabeth St South

Brampton

Ontario.

Someone gave me a turtle.

It was just what I always wanted.

A pet! All my own!

But then I said to myself,

"Where will I keep him?

Where will he live?

He must have a house.

He must have a house all his own."

SO,

I got a hammer.

I got some wood.

I got some nails.

And I built a turtle house.

I put the turtle in it.

He seemed very happy.

But, the next day . . .

My turtle was gone!

He had run away.

So there I was.

There I was with a turtle house

but no turtle to live in it.

What would I do with my house?

Could some other kind of pet

live in it?

"A duck could live in my house,"
I said to myself.
"A duck is a good pet."
SO,
I went down to the pond
to look for a duck.

I found a good one.

I took him home.

But do you know something?

He did not fit in my turtle house.

The house was too small.

SO,

I got the hammer, more wood,

and more nails.

I fixed up the house.

I made it bigger.

Now the house was a duck house.

I put my duck in it.

But do you know what?

That duck was a quacker.

He quacked all day.

He quacked all night.

My mother said the duck must go.

SO,

I swapped him.

I swapped my duck for a kitten.

But did you ever try to put
a kitten in a duck house?
It can't be done.
A duck house is too small.

SO,

I had to go to work again.

I fixed up the house.

I made it bigger.

Now my house was a kitten house.

I put my kitten in it.

He looked mighty happy.

But do you know what?

That kitten ran away, too.

So there I was.

There I was with my house.

No kitten!

No duck! No turtle!

No pet at all!

Then Elmer came by
to give me a rabbit.
I looked him all over.
He looked just right
to fit in my kitten house.

But he didn't fit at all.

I tried and tried to stuff him in.

His back end was just too fat.

SO,

I had to fix up the house again.

Now it was a rabbit house.

I put the rabbit in it.

He looked mighty fine.

But the rabbit made trouble.

He got in my mother's garden.

He gobbled up her flowers.

My mother said the rabbit must go.

SO,

I swapped him.

I swapped the rabbit for a dog.

But did you ever try to put
a dog in a rabbit house?
Don't try it. It doesn't work.
That dog did not fit.
The rabbit house was much too small.

SO . . .

Who had to fix it up?

I had to fix it up.

Now my house was a dog house.

The dog seemed happy.

"At last," I said,

"my troubles are over."

DOG HOUSE

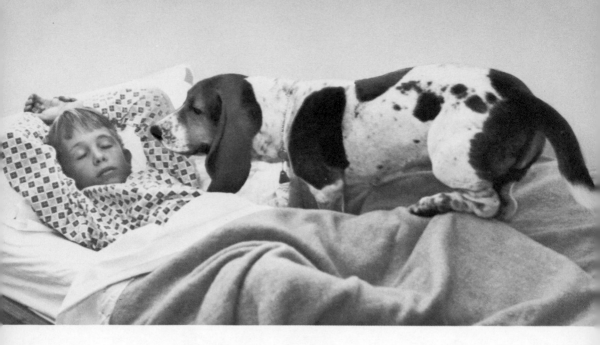

But my troubles were not over.

The dog would not sleep in his house.

Every night he came

into my bed with me.

Mother said he had fleas,

and she gave him away.

So there I was again.

I had no pet at all.

But I had trouble.

Lots of trouble!

I picked up that dog house.

I took it away.

I dumped it.

No more houses!

I was fed up.

No more animals for me!

But about a week later,
I went to Uncle Bert's farm.

Uncle Bert has goats.

Well . . . I began to think of pets again.

I had to have a goat.

I picked out a beauty.

Uncle Bert said I could have her.

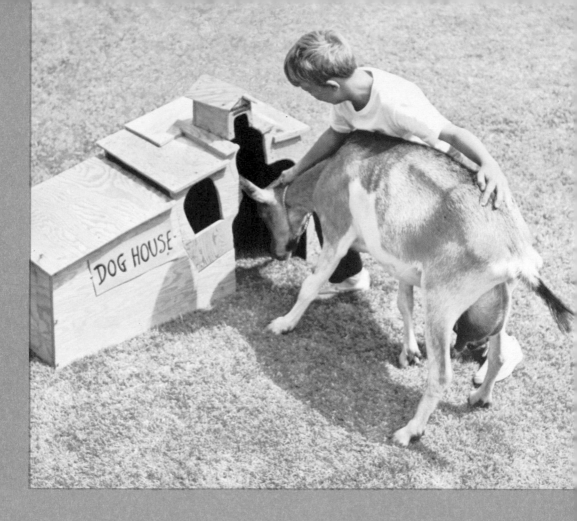

I took her home.

I got the dog house back.

But did you ever try to put

a goat in a dog house?

You can't do it.

A dog house is too small.

SO . . .

That old fixed-up house
had to be fixed up again.
What a job!
It took me two days.

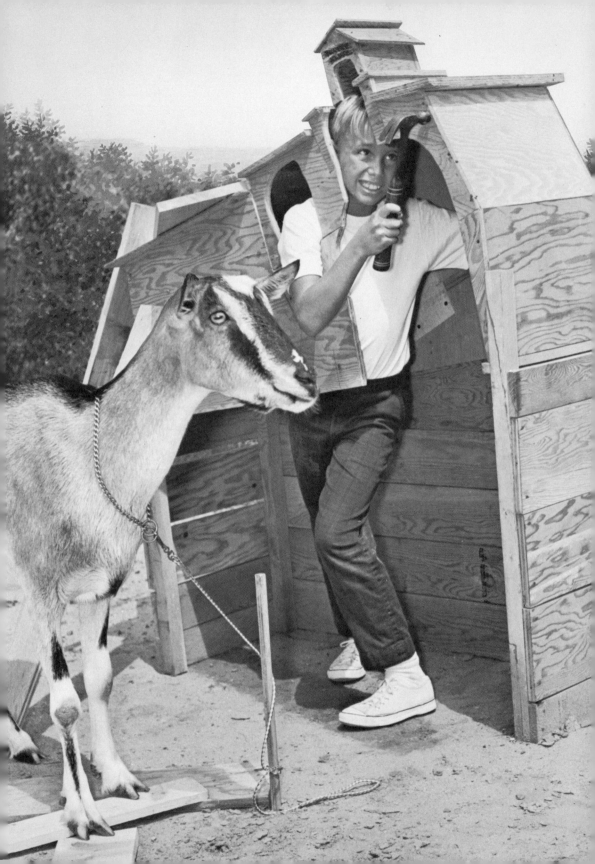

At last the house was done,

and I put the goat in it.

But then . . .

        Do you know what?

GOAT HOUSE

That goat knocked the house down.
Then she jumped on top of it,
and she went "Naa! Naa! Naa!"

I had to take her back to the farm.

But when I was at the farm,

I saw some horses.

How I wanted one!

I picked out a beauty.

Uncle Bert said I could have him.

I rode him home.

I took a look at the house.

What a mess!

Well . . .

I got more wood.

I got more nails.

I got more of everything.

How I worked!

For four long days

I sawed and I hammered.

At last my house was done.

At last my horse was in it.

"Now," I said to myself,

"all my troubles are over!"

But do you know what?

A policeman came around.

"Boy!" he said to me.

"What are you up to?

You can't keep a horse here."

"It's against the law.

Get him out of here. Right now."

I had to take him back to the farm.

So there I was again.

I had fixed up that house

for all kinds of pets.

They had all made trouble . . .

Every one!

Well . . .

I thought about it a long, long time.

Then I laughed. I said,

"I'll fix up my house

for a new kind of pet.

A kind of pet that

will NEVER make trouble!

I'm going to fix up my

house for a BOOGLE."

I don't
quite know
what a
Boogle is.
But one
of these days
I hope
I'll find one.